JONATHAN AND THE BANK ROBBERS

WRITTEN AND ILLUSTRATED BY BEN SHECTER

THE DIAL PRESS NEW YORK

To Joslyn

**ST. BENEDICTS SCHOOL
CAMBRIDGE, OHIO**

"Do I have to go?" pleaded Jonathan. His words were drowned in the stream of Mother's last-minute instructions. The steam from the engine hissed, making his mother and father disappear, along with the glass-domed railway station. Jonathan held tightly to his bag of jelly beans. This was Jonathan's first train trip alone. He was off to visit Uncle Horace, who lived in Cherry Bluffs, the last stop on the New Western Railway. It was a small rail line and all the passengers knew one another.

Jonathan didn't know anyone.

Everyone on the train was talking about the bank robbery that had taken place in Merchantsville, a town along the route. Jonathan listened and munched his jelly beans as they spoke of the daring robbers from the East.

The day was warm and the overhead fans turned lazily as the engine chugged along. Jonathan looked out of the window and watched the summertime countryside follow the train.

"High Falls! Next stop," shouted the conductor.

At High Falls, the town past Merchantsville, a man and woman boarded the train. With arms full of mysterious looking packages and boxes, they settled themselves in the seats opposite Jonathan.

The other passengers looked at them curiously. After a while the woman spoke to Jonathan.

"Are you traveling alone?"

"Yes, ma'am." He spoke up, a bit frightened. "I am going to visit my Uncle Horace."

Some of their packages rattled and clinked, while others remained secretly silent.

"Would you care for a jelly bean?" Jonathan always tried to be polite.

The late afternoon sun grew larger and larger, making everyone on the train look as if he were painted with bright orange-gold.

"Hangstown Junction!" called the conductor.

S-C-R-E-E-C-H, BAM, THUMP! As the train pulled into Hangstown Junction, it suddenly came to an abrupt stop. All the packages and boxes were scattered about. A lid from one of the boxes had fallen off,

revealing something that made Jonathan tremble. The woman quickly placed the lid on the box. She looked at Jonathan and then at the man next to her. Jonathan was terrified by what he had seen. Only bank robbers had black masks!

"There will be a delay," the conductor announced, "because of mechanical difficulties with the engine." He suggested that while the repairs were taking place the passengers wait at the hotel across from the train station.

"Come along with us, dear," said the woman, reaching for Jonathan's hand.

"No, I'd rather stay here." He trembled.

"It's beginning to get dark and it might be a long while before the train can get started again."

If Jonathan could only tell someone what he had seen in the box, and who these people were! While the strange couple busied themselves with their packages and boxes, Jonathan quickly crawled under the seat. Silently he crept along, clutching his bag of jelly beans. He was slipping away from them. Soon he would be out of their reach. Suddenly Jonathan felt something tug at the seat of his trousers, and he was lifted high into the air.

"Young man, this isn't any time for play," scowled the conductor, and he returned Jonathan to his seat. The strange couple, taking everything with them—including Jonathan—left the train.

The Oriental Palace Hotel was big and old with many turrets and spires reaching into the darkening sky. Inside, it was just as

frightening, with winding stairways and dusty chandeliers. Fierce-eyed dragons painted on the ceiling looked down at him. In a dark corner a little elevator descended like a spider into the room. Stepping out to greet them was the oldest woman Jonathan had ever seen. Dressed in flowing Oriental robes, she looked like a Chinese witch.

"Why, Mr. and Mrs. Paradise, what a surprise," she cackled.

"Mrs. McKenzie, how are you?" They exchanged greetings.

Jonathan was horrified that the strange couple and the Chinese witch knew each other. Was this the hide-out of the bank robbers? And were the other passengers walking into a trap? Jonathan was determined to get away from Mr. and Mrs. Paradise as soon as they weren't looking and tell someone about the dangerous situation.

As the other passengers entered the gloomy hotel, the witchlike
lady greeted them with a sly smile pasted on her wrinkled face.
She led them into a dimly lighted dining room, and the little jeweled
bells on her shoes tinkled as she walked.

Mrs. Paradise followed her closely, holding firmly to Jonathan's hand.
Mr. Paradise, leaving the packages and boxes behind, joined them in the
dining room.

Mrs. McKenzie told the passengers that while dinner was being prepared they would all be entertained by lantern slides. The slides were projected on a large white cloth draped on the wall. The image of a moonlit garden on the cloth began to dim, and suddenly the room was

in complete darkness. Jonathan slipped out of the room and ran into
the foyer where the mysterious boxes and packages were. He lifted the
lid off one of the boxes. It was full of swords! "I must warn the
others!" he cried.

Just then Mr. Paradise called "Jonathan!" and came hurrying toward
him. Jonathan stumbled over another box and accidently set free a
swarm of fluttering pigeons in the musty foyer.

"For secret messages!" Jonathan whispered, running up a stairway.
Mr. Paradise didn't follow him, for he was trying to coax the birds
back into the box as they fluttered about the rooms.

Jonathan wandered through long dark hallways and up more winding
stairs. Floors creaked and doors slammed shut. He shivered.
The hotel seemed to be haunted by the ghosts of robbers! Then he saw a pair
of tiny eyes peeking from a shadowy corner, and they flew straight at him.

"Help!" screamed Jonathan as loud as he could and dropped his bag of
jelly beans. Doors suddenly opened and the hotel guests rushed
toward him from all directions, some slipping and tripping on the
jelly beans.

"Good Heavens! What is the matter, child?" a young man said
to him kindly.

A pigeon was perching on Jonathan's head. Someone scooped it up,

and Jonathan quickly told them all about the dangerous bank robbers downstairs.

There wasn't a moment to be lost now.

Arming themselves with umbrellas, walking sticks, and just about anything they could get their hands on, the guests, some in their night clothes, cautiously followed Jonathan down the stairs.

"THERE YOU ARE!" shouted Mr. and Mrs. Paradise.

"That's them, the bank robbers!" cried Jonathan.

With her arms waving like a wounded butterfly, Mrs. McKenzie appeared in the foyer. "What's going on here?" she demanded.

The train passengers looked bewildered and amused at the unusual band of warriors on the stairway. "They've got masks and swords and everything in those boxes," said Jonathan very fast. "They knew I knew about it, and they wouldn't let me out of their sight!"

The train passengers began to laugh. Mr. and Mrs. Paradise and
Mrs. McKenzie laughed the loudest and longest.

"Mr. and Mrs. Paradise are famous magicians," said Mrs. McKenzie.
"They perform in vaudeville shows all over the country and often stay
at my Oriental Palace Hotel."

Jonathan tearfully apologized.

Then the train passengers and the hotel guests all gathered in the dining room for a special magic show to be performed by Mr. and Mrs. Paradise and Company.

The Company was Jonathan, who proved to be a very able assistant. Afterward Mrs. McKenzie permitted Jonathan to ride the elevator up and down four times.

The conductor arrived to say the engine was now ready, and the
passengers reboarded the train.

Jonathan waved good-by to Mr. and Mrs. Paradise from the train

window and thanked them for a new bag of jelly beans. They had decided to stay on for a longer visit with their good friend, Mrs. McKenzie.

The train chugged out of the station. Jonathan sat back drowsily in his seat. He noticed a strange looking man and woman with the oddest black case had gotten on at Hangstown Junction. But Jonathan closed his eyes. Cherry Bluffs wasn't too far away now, and he could hardly wait to see Uncle Horace and tell him about the wonderful bank robbers.

ST. BENEDICTS SCHOOL
CAMBRIDGE, OHIO